Chuckle and Cringe

SpongeBob's Book of Embarrassing Stories

Stephen Hillenburg

Based on the TV series *SpongeBob SquarePants*® created by Stephen Hillenburg as seen on Nickelodeon®

SIMON SPOTLIGHT

An imprint of Simon & Schuster Children's Publishing Division
1230 Avenue of the Americas, New York, New York 10020
© 2007 Viacom International Inc. All rights reserved.
NICKELODEON, *SpongeBob SquarePants*, and all related titles, logos, and characters are registered trademarks of Viacom International Inc. Created by Stephen Hillenburg. All rights reserved, including the right of reproduction in whole or in part in any form.
SIMON SPOTLIGHT and colophon are registered trademarks of Simon & Schuster, Inc.
Manufactured in the United States of America
First Edition
2 4 6 8 10 9 7 5 3 1
ISBN-13: 978-1-4169-4746-2
ISBN-10: 1-4169-4746-9

Chuckle and Cringe

SpongeBob's Book of Embarrassing Stories

by David Lewman

Simon Spotlight/Nickelodeon
New York   London   Toronto   Sydney

SpongeBob NoPants!

by SpongeBob

Life in Bikini Bottom is great! But sometimes it can be a little embarrassing. Like the time I ended up in Mrs. Puff's classroom dressed in nothing but my underwear.

I was getting dressed one morning, and I couldn't decide which belt to wear with my square pants—the black one? Or the other black one?

Just then, Patrick stuck his head through my window. "Hi, SpongeBob!" he called.

"Hi, Patrick!" I answered. "How did you climb up to my window?"

Patrick looked puzzled. "This is *your* window?"

Then he asked if I wanted to go jellyfishing, but I told him I had to go to boating school. And now I was late!

I ran all the way to school, sliding into my chair just in time. The other students were all pointing and laughing. What was so funny? I looked down, and saw that I didn't have on any pants! I'd forgotten to put on my belt, so my pants fell off on the way to school!

Boy, was my face red. And yellow, of course.

Blockhead!

by Patrick

Oh, yeah, I've been *real* embarrassed.

One time I was helping SpongeBob build a new fireplace out of wood. (It ended up not working very well for some reason.) First I helped carry the nails. Then I helped pick up all the nails that had fallen onto the floor, which was all of them. I helped carry boards, too. But when SpongeBob started nailing the boards together, I asked if I could try. He said, "Sure, buddy, but be careful!"

Somehow the very first board I worked on got stuck to my forehead. Which was really embarrassing, because you're not supposed to wear a hat indoors.

The end.

Pirate Day!

by Squidward

I'm embarrassed just about every single day when I go to work at the Krusty Krab. But one day Mr. Krabs managed to make my miserable job even more humiliating than usual.

"It's Pirate Day at the Krusty Krab!" Mr. Krabs announced, grinning.

"What does that mean?" I asked.

"It means you wear this costume," he answered, thrusting a pile of heavy clothes into my hands. "And don't forget to say 'Ahrrr!'"

8

I went into the restroom and put on the clothes Mr. Krabs was forcing me to wear. Then I looked in the mirror. I looked ridiculous! Well, I thought, maybe no one will come to the Krusty Krab today.

But when I walked out of the restroom, there was a huge crowd chanting, "Pirate Day! Pirate Day! Pirate Day!" I guess I should have expected that.

Everyone in Bikini Bottom saw me in that ridiculous, itchy outfit. At the end of that long day, I said, "This shouldn't be called Pirate Day. It should be called Embarrass Squidward Day."

"No, Squidward," said SpongeBob, pointing to a calendar. "That's next Thursday!"

In a Pickle!

by Sandy

I don't get embarrassed easy. Shoot, I'm
from the great state of Texas! What have I
got to be embarrassed about?

But there was one time I had a little . . . accident. As I was leavin' my treedome to go to SpongeBob's house, I grabbed my air helmet. But before I could put it on, it slipped out of my fingers and . . . *crash!*

Now what was I supposed to do? I couldn't just go out in all that water without my helmet!

I ran back into the kitchen, and on the top shelf was a big jar of pickles. If I emptied it, could it work as a temporary air helmet?

I didn't have time to get out my step ladder, so I jumped up, grabbed at the jar—and it fell right on my head!

As the pickles floated past my eyes, I thought, Well, at least no one's here to see this.

But then I heard SpongeBob walk in. "I couldn't wait for you to come over, Sandy, so I decided to come to your house!"

Even the green pickle water couldn't hide my blushin'.

Lucky Penny
by Mr. Krabs

I remember the most embarrassin' thing I ever did. It was when I was just a little baby.

I was crawlin' around, exploring the world. With me claws, I could pick up anythin' that looked interestin' and put it in me blue diaper.

I found a shiny shell and put it in me diaper. A beautiful little grain of sand—into me diaper. A broken bit of coral—into the diaper she goes!

Then, as I was crawlin' along, I spotted somethin' different. It was round, and a little dull, and brown. Should I put it in me diaper? I thought. Nah! It's not shiny and pretty. I crawled on past.

But behind me I heard a bigger boy exclaim, "Oh, boy! A penny!"

It was a penny, and I didn't pick it up! Oh, the terrible shame of it! The only lucky thing was that I was already bright red, so you couldn't see me embarrassment.

Believe me, I never made that mistake again!

Size Matters

by Plankton

Say what you like about me, I don't get embarrassed easily. Furious, yes. Maniacal, certainly. Evil, of course. But not embarrassed.

There is one thing that does embarrass me a little, though. No, not my size! WHAT'S WRONG WITH MY SIZE?! YOU WANT TO MAKE SOMETHING OF IT?!

Sorry. Anyway, there is one tiny embarrassing secret I keep. And it seems to come out at the worst possible times.

Last year, I was attending the annual villains' conference at the convention center in downtown Bikini Bottom. Everybody was there—the Dirty Bubble, Man Ray . . . you name it.

Just as I was about to get up and give my speech, "Keeping Your Evil Plans Fresh," some joker dropped in carrying a big sign with my first name on it and a finger pointing to me. SHELDON, it read. Everyone started to laugh. AT ME!

There's nothing wrong with the name Sheldon. But as a name for a villain . . . well, it doesn't exactly strike terror into the hearts of my victims. I'd just as soon keep it quiet.

I was steaming. Luckily no one could see since I am very, very small.

Stinky Socks

by SpongeBob

Patrick's my best friend, but sometimes his ideas put us right on the express train to Embarrassment City.

Like the time we were trying to think of some good scary costumes for a spooky party. "I know!" shouted Patrick. "We'll be Sockheads!"

"What are Sockheads?" I asked.

"Guys with socks on their heads!" answered Patrick.

"What's scary about that?" I asked.

"Have you ever smelled dirty socks?" Patrick retorted. He grabbed two big, smelly socks and yanked them over our heads.

At the party, people weren't scared of us. In fact, I was pretty sure I could hear them giggling every time we walked by.

But that wasn't the most embarrassing part.

With the sock over my eyes, I couldn't see. Suddenly I felt cold and wet, and I heard a loud crash! I had walked straight into the punch bowl!

We did win a prize, though—for smelliest costume.

Shall We Dance?

by Patrick

SpongeBob's my best friend, but sometimes he has ideas that turn out much different than we expect.

Like the time he thought it would be a nice surprise for Squidward's birthday if we learned to dance the Foxtrot. Whatever that is. I guess it's something Squidward likes.

So we took a ballroom dance class, and we were ready.

We both wore top hats and carried canes to perform at Squidward's party. But we hadn't practiced with the canes. At the end, when we threw our arms in the air, both of our canes went flying! SpongeBob's cane hit Mr. Krabs in the claw, and mine popped three balloons.

Squidward was embarrassed, but SpongeBob and I thought it was pretty funny!

Music to My Ears

by Squidward

SpongeBob has embarrassed me more times than I can count. Like when he and Patrick tried to do some kind of dance for my birthday—puh-leeze!

Or the day I remembered at the last second that it was the annual Bring-a-Guest meeting for Clarinet Club. I was running around begging people to come along—the mail carrier, a policeman, some crazy old lady who was walking by—when SpongeBob overheard me and said he'd love to come along.

I knew it was a terrible idea, but I was desperate. The rules of Clarinet Club are very strict.

We hadn't been at the meeting for more than a minute when SpongeBob started saying I was the best clarinet player in town, and that he knew it was true because I had told him so!

This made the other club members a little peeved.

"Show 'em, Squidward!" SpongeBob exclaimed gleefully. "Play something right now!"

To shut him up, I started to play, but I was so nervous that I made mistake after mistake. I was embarrassed, my teacher was embarrassed—even my clarinet was embarrassed!

But not SpongeBob. "You know, Squidward," he said proudly. "I think that's the best I have ever heard you play!"

Horsin' Around!

by Sandy

Hey, I just remembered another time I got a little bit embarrassed. It was at the Bikini Bottom Rodeo.

I'd been doing great in every event—sea cow herdin', Alaskan bull worm ridin', and giant clam wrestlin'. So I was really looking forward to the ropin' contest.

My lasso was ready to go. I started twirlin' it around, fixin' to toss it over the head of a wild seahorse.

But just as I was startin' to toss my rope, SpongeBob called, "Hi, Sandy!" from the viewin' stands. Without thinkin', I answered, "Hi, SpongeBob!"and waved my hand.

Unfortunately it was my lasso tossin' hand. Instead of goin' around the neck of the seahorse, my lasso went right around the judge of the ropin' contest!

Well, I didn't win that part of the rodeo. And instead of callin' me Sandy Cheeks, you could have called me Red Cheeks!

Money Matters
by Mr. Krabs

I guess it was a wee bit embarrassin' the time I ended up in the Krusty Krab in me pajamas.

For weeks I'd had trouble sleepin'. I spent all night, every night, worryin' that somethin' bad was happenin' to me money.

Finally, one night after frettin' for hours, I counted me money into the dawn. By the time I was done countin', the sun was high in the sky. I was so exhausted that I fell deeply asleep. And I had the most peculiar dream.

I dreamed that I was going for a walk through a beautiful kelp forest where money grew right on the plants. Money had fallen onto the ground all around me, and all I had to do was pick it up!

Suddenly I heard a familiar voice sayin' me name: "Mr. Krabs? Are you all right?" It was SpongeBob!

I woke up and found myself standin' in the Krusty Krab. I'd been sleepwalkin'! Me claws were full of sand I'd picked up, thinking it was money! But even worse: I was standing right in the middle of the dining area, wearin' nothin' but me nightshirt!

I can still hear all the customers laughin'. Still, the humiliation was worth it—what a wonderful dream!

The Rumor Mill

by SpongeBob

One afternoon at work I overheard two customers saying that they'd heard the Krusty Krab was going out of business!

I ran into Mr. Krabs's office. "Mr. Krabs!" I screamed. "Please don't close the Krusty Krab! Please, please, please, please, please!"

Mr. Krabs calmed me down and told me he had no intention of closing his restaurant. "That story, me boy, is just a rumor," he said.

"What's a rumor?" I said. He explained that a rumor was a story spread around as if it were true. "Why do people do that?" I asked. Mr. Krabs said he guessed people thought it was fun.

The next day Patrick and I were sitting around with nothing to do. Patrick said he wanted to do something fun. I remembered what Mr. Krabs had told me, so I suggested we start some rumors.

Patrick and I ran all over Bikini Bottom. "Squidward's head is made of cheese!" we cried.

"Sandy is really a fish in disguise!"

"Mrs. Puff is married to Plankton!"

We told rumors to anyone who would listen—and that was a lot of people!

But it didn't take very long for everybody to trace the rumors back to me and Patrick, and they were real mad at us. Boy, was I embarrassed. I'll never start another rumor again.

Unless maybe it's about myself! Did you know I'm secretly Mermaidman?

THE MAD SCIENTIST

by Plankton

I admit it. One time in high school I was kind of embarrassed.

In chemistry class, we had to figure out what went into this secret formula. I didn't feel like doing it, so I tried to steal the formula from my lab partner, Eugene Krabs. But I got caught, which was embarrassing.

The teacher gave me a failing grade. I vowed I would DESTROY HIM! But I never got around to it.

Come to think of it, admitting this is pretty embarrassing too. Let's just forget the whole thing. Or would you like me to DESTROY YOUR BRAIN?! That's what I thought.

by Mrs. Puff

I like Eugene Krabs—I really do. At the end of a long day of trying to teach SpongeBob how to drive, it's nice to have a quiet, relaxing dinner with Eugene.

But sometimes he can be a little embarrassing.

Last Tuesday, for example, we were in a very nice restaurant, enjoying our desserts. Suddenly one of the other diners dropped a penny. Everyone could hear it rolling across the floor.

Eugene's eyes bugged out. His claws started to click open and closed, faster and faster. Then he dove onto the floor to get the penny!

Everyone stared at him as he grabbed the penny and shouted, "Ah, penny! You've made me the happiest crab in the sea!" Then he started kissing the penny over and over.

And he didn't even leave a tip.

THUMBSUCKERS

by SpongeBob

Once when Patrick and I were out on a walk, he said, "I'm hungry, SpongeBob."

"Sorry," I said. "I don't have any snacks." Then I remembered something. "Hey! Remember when we were little and we'd suck our thumbs? It tasted great!"

"Yeah!" said Patrick, sticking his thumb in his mouth. I sucked my thumb too.

We were walking along, happily sucking our thumbs, when Squidward rode by on his bike. He yelled, "Hey, babies! Want your bottles?"

"Yeah, Squidward! That'd be great!" answered Patrick, smiling and giving a drool-covered thumbs-up.

I was pretty embarrassed. Especially since Squidward called me SpongeBob ThumbSucker for a month.

A Cry for *HELP!*

by Larry the Lobster

As a totally muscular lifeguard, I don't have a lot to be embarrassed about.

But one morning when I was out jogging, I heard someone cry, "Help! Help! I'm going under!"

I realized the distress call was coming from the Krusty Krab, so I burst through the front doors. "Don't worry! Larry the Lobster is here!" I announced. "Who's going under?"

Patrick stuck his head out from underneath a table. "Uh, I am!" he said. "I dropped the toy from my Krusty Meal."

"Then why did you yell 'Help, help'?" I asked.

"It looked kind of dark under there," said Patrick.

I was embarrassed. But *Patrick* should have been embarrassed.

Out of My League

by Squidward

One time in high school I was completely embarrassed in front of a girl I liked.

I was talking to her in the hallway, when my rival, Squilliam Fancyson, came up and started bragging about how he was captain of the chess team.

Before I knew what I was doing, I blurted out, "Oh, yeah? I'm trying out for the football team!"

Squilliam's eyes lit up. "Great!" he said sarcastically. "We'll be there to watch your every move!"

Tryouts were after school that day. And I knew nothing about football! During lunch, I ran into the library and read everything I could about the game.

On the field that afternoon, the coach asked me what position I was trying out for. The only position

I could remember from the book was the quarter-back, so that's what I said.

He shrugged and handed me three balls. "Fine," he said. "Let's see a few passes, Tentacles."

I looked nervously up into the stands. Sure enough, there were Squilliam and the girl I liked. Squilliam cupped his hands around his mouth. "Show us what you got, Squidward!" he yelled.

I picked up the first ball and threw it. It landed about three feet behind me. Squilliam laughed.

I picked up the second ball and tossed it. It hit the coach on the back of his head.

Before he could stop me, I picked up the third football and hurled it as hard as I could. It sailed across the field . . . and right through a gymnasium window! Meanwhile I fell over backward into a big puddle of mud.

Squilliam was laughing so hard he could barely breathe. It was very embarrassing.

But the girl felt so sorry for me that she went out with me for a month!

Ticket to Ride

by Mermaidman

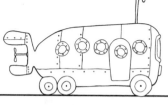

As a superhero it's my job to fight EVIL! But sometimes fighting crime can get a little embarrassing.

Like the time I heard the Sinister Slug was jaywalking in downtown Bikini Bottom. I ran out of the Mermalair and leaped into the Invisible Boat-mobile. Or what I thought was the Invisible Boatmobile, since I landed on the ground with a thud.

I caught a bus downtown and spotted the Sinister Slug. Sure enough, he was crossing the street in the middle of the block!

As I ran toward the fiendish criminal, I tripped over one of my slippers and fell flat on my face. He was getting away!

I dashed across the street, but I forgot to go to the crosswalk, so a policeman gave me a ticket for jaywalking. Needless to say, the Sinister Slug escaped.

ADULT SWIM
by Barnacleboy

Embarrassing stories? I got a million of 'em! But I'm too old to remember 'em.

Except maybe this one. A couple of years ago I decided it had been a long time since I'd gone swimming. I used to do a pretty mean dog paddle. So I headed down to Goo Lagoon.

I arrived just in time for adult swim, which was great. My dog paddle kicks up quite a splash, so I need plenty of room.

But the second I put one toe in the water, I heard the lifeguard's whistle. "What's the problem?" I asked the big, muscular lobster.

"This is adult swim," he answered.

"So?" I snapped back.

"So you're Barnacleboy. During adult swim, no *boys* are allowed in the water!" he barked.

I slunk back to my beach towel and waited until adult swim was over. I may be sixty-eight years old, but I can still blush.

♡ *Puppy Love* ♡

by SpongeBob (and Gary)

My pet snail, Gary, is the greatest pet in history! I take good care of him, so most of the time he's happy. But one time I think he was kind of embarrassed.

I was walking him when he spotted someone walking a beautiful girl snail. Gary tugged on his leash, trying to get over to her. But when Gary reached her, I could tell the beauty of this mollusk made him nervous.

He stood there for a moment, trembling.

Then he coughed up a huge shellball! The girl snail looked disgusted and slid away.

Before that day, I didn't know snails could blush.

All Wrapped Up

by Patrick

One time I was getting ready for a costume party.

I was trying to use this bandage, but I got all tangled up in it.

It was so embarrassing. It completely ruined my mummy costume. The end.

Three Cheers For Pearl!
by Pearl

Last week at school I had a majorly embarrassing day.

I was at cheerleader tryouts, feeling a little nervous. But the coach told me to relax. Because I was on the squad last year, I was pretty sure to make it again this year.

Just then Daddy burst into the gym. "Go, Pearl!" he shouted. "The best little cheerleader in all the Seven Seas!" I thought that was totally humiliating, until he turned to the door and waved his claw. "Okay, come on in!"

"What's going on?" I asked desperately.

Daddy said, "They can't turn down a cheerleader who's got . . . HER OWN CHEERLEADER!"

Suddenly SpongeBob ran in wearing the most ridiculous cheerleading outfit I'd ever seen—baggy tights, a fuzzy headband, and a sweatshirt with my picture on it!

"*P-E-A-R-L* SPELLS 'PEARL'!" SpongeBob screamed. Then he tried to do a cartwheel but slipped on the shiny gym floor and slid right into the bleachers with a crash!

Everyone was pointing and laughing, so to distract them, I did the tryout cheer. The coach congratulated me, and said anyone who could remember a routine through all that chaos definitely belonged on the squad. Whew!

Spin Class
by Sandy

Y'all gotta be real careful when you're exercisin'. Otherwise you just might embarrass yourself.

The other day I was trainin' in my exercise wheel. I decided to really push myself to the limit, so I just kept runnin' faster and faster and faster . . . until the wheel came loose! It started rollin', and took me right out of my treedome, across town, and smack dab into the side of SpongeBob's house!

Not only was I embarrassed, but I got a lot of pineapple juice in my eye. That stuff stings!

Scared Silly

by the Flying Dutchman

It seems like every time I decide to haunt Bikini Bottom, something embarrassing happens!

The last time I sailed me ghostly ship over that little town, I spotted SpongeBob SquarePants out on a walk with his pet snail.

This is a perfect opportunity to scare the daylights out of that little yellow fellow! I thought.

I quickly parked me ship, hopped out, and breathed a mighty blast of fire at the invertebrate. *Har, har!*

Chuckling to myself, I returned to me ship. But I saw there was a ticket on the steering wheel—I'd parked in a loading zone!

Embarrassing? You'd better believe it! Or I'll HAUNT YOU FOR THE REST OF YOUR DAYS! AH HA, HA, HA, HA, HA!

Only kidding. I got better things to do. Like earn some money to pay for this ticket.

HATS OFF!

by Patrick

This one time, I was walking through a dark room. Then suddenly I bumped into someone.

"Excuse me," I said. No one said anything back.

"I said, 'Excuse me,'" I repeated. Still nothing. How rude!

So I started a big fight. Grabbing, shaking, growling—the whole bit.

Turns out I was fighting a hat rack.

And I lost.

Burst Your Bubble

by the Dirty Bubble

You know, people think supervillains never get embarrassed, but it's not true. We do.

Once I was right in the middle of a big fight with Mermaidman and Barnacleboy, and I was sure I was going to win.

But just as I was about to deliver the final blow, something really embarrassing happened.

I popped.

By the time I got myself reinflated, they'd thrown me in jail. And everyone could see my dirty blushes.

Candid Camera
by SpongeBob

This is a really embarrassing picture of me from a party.

I can't remember how my pants fell down or why I'm wearing my protective karate headgear.

All I know is, I hope no one has a copy of this picture, especially hidden in some secret box.

Wait a minute! Now *you* have a copy! Oh, no!

I'M WITH THE DUMMY!

by Patrick

I bought this really great shirt. It was so funny!

But then when I wore it, I was really embarrassed.

Why, you ask? I will tell you, gentle reader.

Because I realized that everyone I was hanging out with was a dummy!

Well, I guess that's enough stories for now. As you can see, embarrassing things happen to everyone, so it's okay to feel embarrassed now and then.

After all, no one's perfect *all* the time!

I BEG TO DIFFER!